The

Innkeepers

H. Rad Bethlen

Rooster & Raven

For the Daughters of Zeus and Mnemosyne

Author Statement Concerning Artificial Intelligence

The way I write consist of several phases.

1. Idea generation.
2. Research.
3. Story development.
4. Outlining.
5. Writing the rough draft.
6. Editing and rewriting.
7. Editing and polishing.
8. Copy editing.

I will *occasionally* use AI during the research phase if I can't locate some bit of information on my own—but I try to locate it on my own first.

I will *occasionally* use AI during the story's development if I get stuck on something—but I try to resolve my own story issues first.

I *intentionally* use AI during the copy editing phase as a stand-in for a copy editor, which I can't afford to pay for yet which I don't want to go without.

A copy editor is the last set of eyes to look at a manuscript to check for grammar, usage, spelling, and punctuation mistakes. I ask the AI copy editor to make suggestions on corrections. I evaluate those suggestions. If I agree, I make the changes.

I don't use AI for anything else.

Be comforted that these stories were written by a human being for other human beings.

H. Rad Bethlen

The Innkeepers - Eternal Rest

A group of innkeepers in a fair-sized city had formed a guild. This was really a price-fixing scheme, which they dignified with offices and dues. They met in the taproom of a public house in order to spend those dues and decide, to their mutual benefit, the "fair market value" of what they had to rent. With this new business concluded, they resumed the old, the telling of tall tales and the ridicule of those whom they had fleeced.

"I ask," began a not-too-proud dwarven man by the name of Reynard. He was an honorable dwarf, as are so many of his race. The honor he kept foremost was this: it was, as he understood it, "*dis*honorable to let a fool keep his money." You might note his charming take on that old adage.

"Would you turn away coin if the bearer displeased you?" Reynard continued. "There are so many types, all looking stranger than the last. Aye, one doesn't know what to make of them. Why, just yesterday I had a dark elf attempt to claim my best room for a week! And this," he pounded the table with his fist, sloshing the ale in the guild members' flagons, "given the despicable and egregious wrongs his race has done to mine!"

"Answer your own question, Reynard," said Tybalt, a whimsical half-elven bard who had purchased an inn for the captive audience it provided. "Did you put him out with a swift boot?"

A smile raised the dwarf's red mustache and made his thickly-plaited beard tremble. "Put him out? Why, he's there now! Sleeping like a baby! I charged him triple, mind you, deeming it just." He howled at his own capriciousness and added, as if it needed adding, "Drow coin spends as well from my purse as any other!"

"But *is* he handsome?" asked Dame Bellyn, the only lady of the guild, and a proper Lady at that, even though she "slummed" with the mercantile set.

"I've a mind to speak to yer husband on that point, Madam," growled Reynard, with a wink.

"Please do," countered Dame Bellyn. "I should like him found. He's off on another expedition, leaving me to oversee his various interests. Why he feels the wild expanse," she waved a ring-laden hand to take in the whole of the unknown corners of the globe, "requires illumination baffles me. I received a letter stating that his chief cartographer had been melted by acid from the mouth of a black dragon. Melted! I couldn't finish the letter. Oh, the way he dropped that on me, it was scandalous!"

After the laughter had quieted down, 'Gray' Kell, a dark-haired, long-faced, narrow-framed, human, although some questioned that, on account of the grayish tint to his skin, the source of his moniker, who, in addition, may or may not be involved with the local thieves' guild, raised a finger. The other innkeepers looked at him. "The question is," he began, looking at Reynard, "not whom would you turn away, but whom would you gladly accept above all others?"

"Adventurers!" cried the group in unison, all except one, a man named Rucklan.

Gam, a gnome, who sat in a high-backed stool to keep him at eye-level with his peers, picked up the thread. "Have I told you about the time I convinced a group of adventurers to leave behind all their surplus gear and loot in my care whilst they went off to the nearest dungeon? They never returned!" The gnome laughed. The rest of the group, except for Dame Bellyn, frowned at his good fortune.

"Perhaps once too often," observed Tybalt.

"I've one for you," said Rucklan, or simply, "Ruck," who had yet to speak. By all appearances he was a human man in his middle years, stout and hearty, with his chestnut-colored hair combed back and a thick mustache that fell over his top lip, hiding it from view. Ruck knew better than most that in this world one cannot go on appearances alone. "This happened quite some time ago," he began. "Before I was the owner of the finest inn—"

"Hey!"

"Careful!"

"'Finest', humph!"

Ruck held up his hands. "*One* of the finest?"

The guild agreed to the new terms.

"I was working for one of our own. I was but a lad and he was a blackguard to his very bones—"

"It was him that taught ye, eh?" asked Reynard.

"By harsh lessons alone, yes," said Ruck. "He was the owner of the only inn on a stretch of lonesome road. He felt a town would spring up around him. He was disappointed. Nonetheless, some are blessed with fortune where nature has left them short on intelligence.

"He had come upon a dilapidated building in his wanderings and had taken a fancy to its stones and the carvings thereon, which, on occasion, flashed with the glow of ancient magic. He had a bit of coin, this blackguard, no doubt earned by honest means," to this the group laughed. "Finding a source of clean water nearby and noticing that the road was in good repair, a sign he took as evidence of its regular use, he added wood to the stones and arrived at an inn of which we would all be proud. He hung a shingle painted with two hares frolicking. So the inn became known as the Frolicking Hares or the Two Hares, or the Hares, depending on the interpreter."

Ruck took a drink of ale and continued. "At first he was dismayed. Not a single traveler passed by for days. He had trouble even finding someone to employ. He went out to the road, looking this way and that," Ruck swiveled his head. "He looked down beneath his feet." Ruck mimicked his former employer, then looked at his peers and resumed his tale. "He found, under the dust of time, cut stones. The road *had* been well cared for, a century prior.

"He spent his time admiring the carvings on his own stones, lamenting his bad fortune, and getting drunk on what beer he'd brewed from the wild hops near at hand. He admired the bluish glow that played along the stones and wondered at the old enchantment. He wondered if they were valuable, these stones, then despaired at the labor of transporting them. He was about to give up the enterprise altogether when he was 'discovered.' I should say that the ruins all around him were discovered. He had unknowingly rebuilt the only visible remains of an ancient city, long forgotten by time and almost reclaimed by nature.

"As it so happens some over-curious young lady toiling away in one of those lofty wizard's towers came across an ancient tome that spoke of the wonders of said city. Her mentor, herself, and a few others, armed and armored, went in search of this marvelous place that time forgot. What did they find? Why, Frolicking Hares. Believe me, they were straight put out. They thought someone had beaten them to it. They soon came to the realization they had an idiot on their hands.

"He was a useful idiot, however," continued Rucklan. "The wizards were all set to open some pocket dimension in which they could 'rough it'. They saved their scrolls and opted instead for clean linens. My master was pleased. Here were paying customers.

They enlightened him as to the true nature of the hills and valleys thereabout. This made sense of the strange stones. The adventurers did some poking about, realized the ruins were not only immense but were also quite dangerous, and after some time and the loss of one of their number, returned from whence they came.

"My, at that point future, employer locked the doors, went to the nearest town, and spread the news. Magic-filled ruins! Priceless treasures awaiting the adventurous! You know—marketing. He hired a few pitiful souls to serve and clean, myself included. We returned to the Hares and awaited the rush of adventurers seeking fortune and fame. Weeks passed. Then months. We had a few visitors, sure, traders passing through. We told them of the ruins. 'More ruins? Humph!' Was the usual response.

"Again my man was close to locking the doors and losing the key. We were at each other's throats and were turning into right proper savages under the negative influence of boredom. Then an adventuring party showed up and saved the day. We hopped-to and made them feel like great heroes of myth. They went into the ruins, came out the worse for it, and left our good graces. Word spread. Before long, we had a full house. The hares were frolicking indeed!

"The ruins welcomed any who would dare. We didn't bother to remember our adventurers' names, there were so many, and so many never came out. I mean, why bother getting to know them? But," he paused for effect, "one did come out, you see. He was old, older than Reynard here—"

"Careful," growled the dwarf.

"He looked a sight. Perhaps you've heard tales of men or women hit by certain necromantic spells that rob them of their vitality. Either this poor man had just such an experience or he had lost it honestly. Had he stayed at the

Hares on his way in? I racked my memory for his face, it was one that would stick. If so, how long ago? Had he gone in full of verve only to stagger out blighted by necromancy? He took a room, speaking only to the owner, and disappearing to slumber despite the early hour.

"He didn't dine in the common room that evening nor the next morning. Point of fact, we all forgot about him as just then a massive adventuring group crossed our doorstep. They had come to do the ruins justice. They had one of everything! They put us to task and we had to hop quick to get them all fed and watered.

"Later that evening I was out front, catching my breath, when a lone traveler came down the road. He was a merchant by the looks of him. He stopped his cart and asked me if there was a room. I doubted it but I fetched the master anyway. He came out and this is the conversation they had:

"'Do you have a room?'" asked the merchant.

"'I've a bed.' Said my master.

"'Is there another inn?' asked the merchant, to which my master scoffed. 'A bed, what do you mean?' Asked the merchant, seeing his prospects limited.

"'A double room.' Said my master. Now, we had two double rooms," said Ruck. "I knew that the adventurers just arrived had claimed one. I was at a loss as to who had the other. Then I remembered the man who had come out of the ruins. My master must have thrust the double room on him, to earn a premium.

"'And the man occupying the other bed?' Asked the merchant.

"'As quiet as a mouse.' Said my master. 'He won't disturb you in any way. Of that I'm certain. I have yet to meet a quieter man.'

"'His character?' Asked the merchant.

"'At peace, I should surmise.' Said my master, with a bit of a smirk.

"'Well, then, I shall take the bed for the night.' Said the merchant, descending from his cart and taking his coin purse from his coat pocket. He produced a few coins and held them out. My master paused. I'd never seen him hesitate to take money into his hands. That drew my attention.

"'There's one stipulation,' began my master. 'This is the last I have to rent and demand for it is certain. I can offer you no refund should the bed or your companion not be to your liking.' This set the merchant on guard.

"'You said the man was quiet and peaceful. What should I find disagreeable about his company?' Asked the merchant. To this my master shrugged his shoulders.

"'Only know I offer no refund.'

"'Fair enough,' said the merchant." Ruck took another sip and continued. "The road had wearied our fair merchant as had the negotiations. He was ready for a mug of ale and a night's rest. I took his bags and followed him and my master to the double room. The current occupant, the man I described earlier, was in his bed, already asleep, or so it seemed. Night was coming on and the light in the room was dim. We hadn't brought a candle. The merchant made a survey of the room under those conditions. I entered and set his bags next to the vacant bed. In the other bed lie the man, the blanket pulled over his head. Perhaps this was to blot out what little light there was or perhaps he was aware of the effect his visage had on those who gazed upon him. Whatever the reason, I was glad.

"'Seems an odd chap,' observed the merchant. 'How can he breathe, I wonder?'

"'To each his own.' Said my master. We bade our most recent guest good night and went downstairs. There was a bit more serving and cleaning to be done then we all went to bed ourselves, only to be awoken by a man bounding down the stairs, screaming. I was the first to meet him in the hall.

"'Dead!' the merchant cried. 'He's dead!'

"I went at once to rouse the master. He eyed me and said, 'remember I offer no refunds in this case.' We all went upstairs. The merchant had annoyed the other guests. My master worked to console them. I went with the merchant to the double room. The blanket had been thrown back to reveal the gaunt, bone-white, and death-stilled face of his roommate.

"'I noticed his blanket neither rose nor fell. I had to check on the poor fellow,' the merchant said to justify his curiosity. I went to the man," said Ruck, "and, despite my fear, examined him. I had a candle with me. I had lit it upon first hearing the cry of 'dead'. I held it to the man's face. The flame did not waver. That man pushed no air from his lungs. His condition now matched his appearance. My master stood in the doorway.

"'What's the meaning of this?' Demanded the merchant.

"'You wanted a bed and you got one.' Said my master. He stepped in and went to the corpse. 'I trust he did not disturb your slumber.' He said, chuckling. He returned the blanket to its previous state, covering the dead man's face.

"'He did!' Cried the merchant. 'How could a man sleep in the presence of a corpse?' Receiving no reply he continued. 'You knew full well he was dead, didn't you? That is why you offered no refund. You, Sir, are—.'

"My master spun. 'You've never taken a customer, eh? You've never used guile to earn a bit extra when you've suspected you had the advantage?' At this my master laughed. He looked from the merchant to the now-fully-covered corpse, 'Yes, I knew he was dead. I came to offer him breakfast and found him like you see him now. I suspect he knew his time was approaching and desired a soft bed to die in. I was going to toss him but then we got busy and I hadn't the time. You came along and wanted a bed.' He now looked at the merchant. 'I gave you what you wanted.'

"'Only you failed to mention my sleeping companion was beyond sleep.' Said the merchant. My master shrugged."

At this Ruck paused.

"Just then," he continued, "the blanket covering the dead man shuddered. The bed creaked. The sound, so natural, yet so unexpected, ended the argument. Everyone in the room, myself, my master, and the merchant, looked at the sheet-covered-corpse. *Had* the bed creaked? *Had* the blanket been disturbed by some movement from beneath? Or were our ears and the candle light playing us false? We watched, each of us holding our breath tight within our chests. The bed creaked again! Something moved beneath the blanket! The dead-man's arm was seen bending at the elbow. It moved with exaggerated slowness, from his side, across his chest, then higher.

"We watched as his pale, emaciated hand crept into view at the top of the blanket. The knob-knuckled fingers curled and gripped the edge of that covering. The arm rose and descended, pulling the cover down, revealing the dead man's head and shoulders. His eyes were closed, his face the very the likeness of that Horseman he had certainly met. The arm finished its arc, coming to rest again at his side, having pulled the blanket to his waist.

"We would have screamed, if we had the presence to. We had seen the dead move. That alone took the breath from us. What followed finished us. The eyes opened! The head rotated until those milked-over orbs came to rest upon us. The dry, withered lips parted, revealing gray, shrunken gums, and time-blackened teeth, barely anchored. A deep voice, made deeper perhaps by issuing forth from the grave, said, 'Would you kindly keep it down.'"

The other guild members blinked in astonishment and looked to each other for answers. They returned to their storyteller. He smiled.

"The man *was* dead," he explained. "Had been dead from the first. Had been dead, it turns out, for well over a century. His peaceful slumber within his crypt deep within the ruins had been disturbed by the influx of adventurers. He had decided to abandon his former home in search of somewhere further removed from society. This he told us himself, when he asked for a full refund and prepared to take his leave."

At this the guild was incredulous. They made accusations of poor play. They demanded to know whether the tale was to be believed or whether he was having a bit of sport on their part.

"I'll tell you this," Ruck said, in conclusion. "My master gave the dead man his refund, without squabbling, and I decided then and there two things that would shape my life forever after. First, I was *not* going to be an adventurer, no matter the potential riches, and second, I was *never* going to cater to adventurers or their ilk. It's not worth the trouble."

The Innkeepers - A Voice so Pure

A group of innkeepers in a fair-sized city had formed a guild. This was really a price-fixing scheme, which they dignified with offices and dues. They met in the taproom of a public house in order to spend those dues and decide, to their mutual benefit, the "fair market value" of what they had to rent. With this new business concluded, they resumed the old, the telling of tall tales and the ridicule of those whom they had fleeced.

The innkeepers were: Tybalt, the bard; "Gray" Kell, called so because of the tint of his skin, pointing, perhaps, to otherworldly origins, despite his claims to the contrary; the red-haired dwarf, Reynard; the sole lady of the group —a proper Lady at that—Dame Bellyn; the gnome, Gam; and finally Rucklan. With guild business concluded and much ale drunk, they now began their beloved pastime, the telling of tall tales.

"Would you believe," began Tybalt, "that mine is not the clearest soprano occupying all points of the compass?"

At this question Gam, perched in a high-backed stool, to keep him at eye-level with his peers, tilted his head. "Soprano?" He raised an eyebrow and looked over the guild, "A weak tenor, perhaps, with an uneven falsetto?"

"What do your ears know?" shot Tybalt. "Look at the shape of them, everything you perceive must be attenuated by that." He reached out and ran a fingertip along the ample stretch.

"Your breeding shows," said Dame Bellyn, chastising the bard.

"Ah, let the man speak," said Reynard. "If we begin on ears, the gnome will keep about it for days. I'm certain one of his many middle names means 'he of long ears.'"

"That would be fifth from—"

"See!" growled Reynard.

"If only I'd settled in a different town," lamented Kell.

"Oh, hush," said Dame Bellyn, "besides, who would run the thieves' guild, if not you?"

Kell raised a finger of protest and was about to speak but shut his mouth and let the question go unanswered.

"The unqualified finest soprano I've ever had the chagrin to hear belonged to a," here Tybalt paused, debating the best adjective. He went for obscuration instead of clarification, "a—unique—bard, named Mugho."

"Sounds goblinoid," grumbled Reynard.

Tybalt looked at the dwarf, then away.

"At least your ego allows one above you," said Kell.

Tybalt eyed him. "My ego aside, the ear proves the truth of it." He looked sidelong at Gam, "in most cases."

"Jealous?" asked Gam.

"I think not," replied Tybalt. He was half-elven and thus did have pointed ears but not near the length of his gnomish friend.

"Mugho," said Rucklan, "following you so far."

Tybalt took a sip of his ale and continued. "There is many a country seat occupied by a rough and tumble class. They erect castles and oppress the peasantry best they know how."

Dame Bellyn laughed. This earned her a few curious looks.

"Cousins," she said by way of dismissal.

"I was just getting settled into one such country seat," continued Tybalt, "when our story takes place. A fine little post. The Lord in question was of the muddy-boot and bloody-blade type."

"Aye!" said Reynard. He raised his mug to the unknown knight.

"Under the cultured influence of his new, and much younger, bride—"

"Aye!" said Reynard again, drinking to young brides. This brought a round of laughter from the guild and a smirk from Tybalt.

"He was laboring towards refinement," continued the half-elf. "He had two daughters from a previous marriage, one engaged and soon to be married herself, and one younger, afflicted by blindness."

"Oh, poor thing," said Dame Bellyn.

"Not so," said Tybalt. "For she had developed a marvelous ear and could sing with real skill, her voice diminished only by a lack of confidence. I secured my newfound post thanks to her appreciation of music, as I was to not only to perform for the modest court, but instruct her as well. As you can imagine, I thought myself secure, but due to the forthcoming ceremonies, Sir Scott," he glanced at Reynard, "that's your man's name."

"A right-minded man, except for all this culture nonsense," said Reynard.

Tybalt raised an eyebrow. "Nevertheless, your man decided to hold a contest to determine who shall sing at the wedding."

"Ah," said Gam, "his ears—"

"Not one," said Tybalt, speaking over the gnome, "to shy away from competition, I was all for such a contest."

The guild, save Tybalt, shared a chuckle and a knowing look.

"'Let them come,' said I, 'from far and wide. My voice can hold its own and my lute-play sparkles in the light of competition.'"

"Aye," said Reynard. "That's the spirit, lad."

"Thank you, my dear friend," said Tybalt. "Wench, top-off my good companion's mug, shall you?"

The barmaid, familiar with the antics of the group, brought over a pair of pitchers and saw that each mug was refreshed.

Tybalt leaned forward and continued in a conspiratorial tone. "Once the competition was announced, I immediately got on good terms with the cooks and serving maids of the place."

"Poison?" asked Kell, a bit too unabashedly for comfort. He noticed the stares. "What?"

"Not everyone thinks first of murder," said Dame Bellyn.

"I didn't say—"

"Along the right lines, though," said Rucklan, looking at Tybalt. "Is he not?"

"Indigestion has ruined more than one performance," said Tybalt. He sat back. "Word spread, drawing a flood of hopefuls like flotsam. Some had talent, but I had cunning—often the sharper edge. I was the one to topple over, you see, being established, as I was. I began to size up my competition. No doubt a few had the promise of talent but I had cunning and that's often more than enough of an equalizer in these circumstances.

"More than a dozen of my peers filtered in over a fortnight. The day of the competition was fast approaching. The night before the contest one last hopeful showed his," here he looked at Reynard, "filthy, green-skinned head."

"I knew it!" said the dwarf, banging his fist on the table. "A goblin?"

"Indeed," said Tybalt. "How a goblin had heard of the contest and how he came to the castle—alone," Tybalt frowned, "who knows. But arrive he did. He spoke the common tongue well enough to be understood, if one had patience. The whole lot of us were seated in the great hall; which, mind you, wasn't *that* great, when a manservant announced the arrival of a competitor. We all turned in time to see this Mugho chap stride confidently in."

"Sir Scott took up arms, yes?" asked Reynard.

"We were all too stunned to do much of anything." Said Tybalt. "Why, the temerity of this goblin was not to be believed. What's worse, he had a sort-of lute, a travesty, with one string. Who knows out of what garbage pile he'd rescued it."

"I love this little fellow already," said Dame Bellyn.

"He's got pluck," agreed "Gray" Kell.

"Sometimes that's enough," added Rucklan.

"Oh? He'll be warmed to know the guild supports his antics," said Tybalt. "Shall I continue or do you require more time to sing his praises?"

"A bit touchy on the point," said Gam.

"After our initial shock passed, the entire room, save one, burst out in uproarious laughter," said Tybalt.

"Oh, poor thing," said Dame Bellyn. "You probably hurt his feelings."

"Don't have 'em," said Reynard.

"I'm certain they do," said Bellyn.

"No, really." Reynard placed a hand over his heart and shook his head. "Vacant of—"

"The one on whom the joke was lost," continued Tybalt, "was Anne, the blind daughter. I happened to be seated next to her. She felt for my arm and when she found it she inquired as to the cause of the merriment. I was about to inform her when her father spoke.

"'Bring the good little fellow forward,' he commanded his manservant. The goblin was brought to the front. 'You wish to compete?' Asked Sir Scott. The goblin nodded. 'You can sing?' Asked Sir Scott's wife, Lady Melinda. Mugho, we would later learn his name, nodded again. 'Recite poetry?' Asked the Lady. The goblin nodded. 'I see also that you have a lute.' Said the Lady. This Mugho fellow displayed his pride and joy. This, as you can imagine, brought another round of laughter.

"I yet again attempted to explain the situation to Anne but when I turned I saw she was retiring from the hall, led out with the help of her handmaiden. I imagine as one sensitive to insult she wished not to participate in what was becoming a grand jest on this poor little fellow's behalf."

"I'm telling you," interjected Reynard, "goblins have no feelings whatsoever."

"Hush," said Dame Bellyn, frowning at the dwarf. "Go on," she said to Tybalt.

"'Dancing?' asked Sir Scott. 'A fine dancer he is, I'm sure of it!' The goblin bowed. Sir Scott leaned forward. He seemed to grow serious. He looked over the faces of his court. We knew not what to expect and fell silent. He looked back at the goblin. 'Juggling?' He asked with exaggerated pathos, as if he'd long suffered for the lack of a juggler in his court."

"That's just mean," said Dame Bellyn.

"Mugho seemed not to know the word. His green brow pinched over his large, black eyes. 'You can't juggle?' Asked Sir Scott, feigning heartbreak. It was clear the goblin was at a loss. Sir Scott, full in the mood, rose, took up several rolls, stepped around the table, and attempted to juggle. He made a mockery of the art. When each roll was dirtied from multiple missed catches he hung his head." Tybalt smiled.

"Mugho," Tybalt looked at Reynard, "despite your claims to the contrary, was full of empathy. He reached out, patted Sir Scott on his thigh, picked up the rolls and did his best to accomplish what the knight could not. Of course, having never tried before, he fared little better.

However, seeing the goblin was a ready sort of fellow, a series of similar jest ensued. Before the evening was over we had him walking on his hands while balancing the crockery on the bottoms of his feet. We were worn out from laughter and all slept well, I assure you."

Tybalt wetted his throat and continued.

"The next morning began the competition. I had conspired with some of the help to give myself an edge. Breakfast found me short of appetite." Here he laughed. "My competition ate heartily."

"The best poisons are the sweetest," observed "Gray" Kell.

"This is why I refuse to dine in your establishment," said Dame Bellyn.

"I would never harm a fellow guild member," said Kell.

"Humph!" exclaimed Dame Bellyn.

"When Sir Scott and Lady Melinda came down from their chambers we had another laugh," said Tybalt. "The lady had sewn a jester's cap for Mugho."

"No," said Dame Bellyn.

"Yes," said Tybalt. "Mugho didn't recognize it for what it was. When the lady placed it on his oversized head with all due ceremony he thought it was a great honor. It was the cleanest article of clothing in his possession.

"What I want to know," said Gam, "is did you poison this Mugho as well? That is, were you threatened by *him*?"

"I—" began Tybalt, only to be interrupted by Reynard.

"Wouldn't do no good. If you knew what goblins ate." The dwarf shook his head. "Poison would hardly slow 'em down. An axe, however, an axe—"

"Thank you for your insights," said Dame Bellyn. "I do hope this story has a happy ending," she added, looking hard at Tybalt.

"Happy for *me*?" he asked. He knew her desire, however, and reassured her with a smile. "The day began. I paid no more attention to Mugho. He was no threat, or so I thought. I missed the tragedy that was his lute play. I missed the confusion that was his poetry recital. He had, apparently, stayed up all night practicing juggling and I heard from others that he delighted Sir Scott with an admirable display."

"Told you he has pluck," said "Gray" Kell.

"He's a ready fellow," added Rucklan.

"He's the hero of our story, I assure you," said Tybalt. "Or the villain, if you happened to be on *my* side." Here the guild fell mute. "As I thought," grumbled Tybalt. "The highlight of the competition, that is, the most important contest, was an unaccompanied performance before the bride and her sister. It was Anne's keen ears that would ultimately decide. I had held my own throughout the day, owing no doubt to the thoughtful application of various poisonous herbs to my competition's breakfast and lunch."

At this "Gray" Kell smirked.

"Each performer went before the sisters," said Tybalt. "Each applied him or herself as best they could. The faces of the judges gave away nothing. They were about to retire for consideration when, from above, a sorrowful melody drifted down—raw, haunting, piercing the air until tears stung our eyes. I swear to you even the hens in the courtyard ceased their clucking and scratching out of respect. All ears turned upwards.

"Who owned this miraculous voice? Mugho. He had realized the jest being shamelessly perpetrated on him. He'd gotten wise but, perhaps by orders of Sir Scott, he was kept from the contest. I don't wonder if he was invited to leave the grounds under penalty of death.

"Mugho was standing atop the battlements, having climbed the exterior wall. He had discarded, or lost, his jester's cap and wore his familiar rags and tattered cloak. The sight of him was curious, unbelievable, really, but if one closed his eyes and listened." Tybalt shook his head. "Really, words fail."

"What happened next?" asked Dame Bellyn, leaning forward.

"Anne wept," said Tybalt. "Oh, she wasn't the only one. I admit that the beauty of his voice touched me as well. When the song ended, oh, it ended far too soon, we knew we'd been licked. How could we compete? As a jester he was a failure. As a singer he was supreme." Tybalt sat back. "I had done all I could to emerge victorious," he said. "I had even compromised my morals."

"Humph!" emitted Reynard.

The guild smirked in agreement.

Even Tybalt had to smile.

"I learned a valuable lesson that day," he said. "I'd dismissed him as a jest, yet there he stood, voice soaring where mine faltered—a humbling tune indeed."

Dame Bellyn dabbed her eyes with her kerchief.

"We were all ashamed and embarrassed," said Tybalt. "Myself most of all, for I had thought so little of Mugho as to not even consider him a rival and yet who do you imagine sang at the wedding?" Tybalt smiled. "He made a fine sight in a doublet and hose."

"To Mugho," said Reynard, lifting his mug. "A ready fellow indeed."

"Hear! Hear!" said the guild in unison.

Do Goblins Love?

The children fought over a bone, growling and hissing. They formed a writhing mass, linked by their grip on the bone. They bumped into Vashti, their mother. She hissed at them and bared her teeth. The biggest child yanked at the bone, hurling the smaller ones against the few upright objects in the kitchen.

Vashti struggled to recall if the biggest child was hers. She probed her faltering memory for his origins but came up empty. Standing on her toes, she reached onto the table, feeling for another bone. She found one and tossed it into the corner. The children, despite their clamor, caught the sound. They broke apart and swarmed the second bone.

The smallest of her brood cowered beneath the table, eyes fixed on her. Vashti reached out, seized the child, and dragged her across the room, through a hole in the wall to a small, dark nook. They huddled together, peering out. The other children eventually gnawed the bones to pieces and ate them. The wild pack then scoured the kitchen, sniffing, rooting through filth, and clambering over each other. Finding nothing, they wandered off.

Sometime later a male came. Vashti could hear him sniffing the air. He passed through her field of vision, not looking into the hole. He went to the corner where the bones had been. She could hear his claws scraping against the stone floor.

He passed again, stopped, sniffed the air, and turned towards her and her daughter. He approached, stopped in front of the hole, and sniffed. He peered into the darkness. She could see his eyes glow in the dim light that came from one of the two hallways. He stuck his head into the small space, followed by his arm. He felt around, touching first Vashti, then her daughter. He felt their clothing, found their pockets, and searched them. He pulled his hand out of the small space.

"Food?"

Vashti shook her head. The male sniffed. He looked at the girl. Vashti growled. He looked at her. She curled her lips, showing her teeth. He pulled back from the nook and disappeared from sight.

When her daughter fell asleep, Vashti slipped from the nook. She dragged the table over, flipped it onto its side, and wedged it against the hole. She checked both hallways, finding them empty. Sniffing the air, she closed her eyes to listen, then returned to the kitchen.

She moved one of the chairs against the wall. She stepped up onto it, testing it, balancing. She climbed from the chair onto the black metal box. She did not know it was a cast-iron stove. She only knew it was empty and could not be moved. She climbed from the stove to a shelf. The wood creaked. She stopped. She listened. She continued. At the far end of the shelf she reached up. She found a loose stone and pulled it free.

She looked around. She sniffed the air. She listened. Secure in her privacy, she reached into the space that lay behind the stone. Her clawed fingers touched the strange object. She had no term for it. She pulled it free. She set it on the shelf in front of her and opened it. The image of a man was so careful drawn it seemed alive. Even though the man had never moved, seemed trapped, somehow, in a way she couldn't understand, Vashti still feared him.

She lifted the page and peered beneath it, but he wasn't there—only rows of black marks. She let the page drop, rubbed her fingertips on her patched dress, and checked their cleanliness before touching the man's image. She found him beautiful: his muscles, his long flowing hair, the firm set of his jaw, and especially his almond-shaped eyes.

A noise reached her ears. She snapped the book shut, shoved it back into the hole, reset the stone, and scrambled down to the floor. Her daughter pushed the table out, just far enough to slip past. She scanned the kitchen, then glanced at her mother descending from the stove.

Vashti saw hunger glinting in her daughter's eyes. She felt it too, though she'd grown accustomed to the ache. She growled and waved her arms to scold her. The girl shrank back, clutching the table for cover, yet held her mother's gaze. Guilt stirred in Vashti. She stepped closer, touched her daughter's face, then seized her wrist and pulled her from behind the table. Together, they left the kitchen to hunt for food.

. . .

Vashti and the children, all but the largest, huddled in the small space. The largest slept in the unused stove. Vashti was half asleep. Noises brought her to full wakefulness. She pushed the table out of the way.

Several males dashed through the kitchen. The children squirmed, and Vashti drew them closer. She began dragging the table back to shield them, but a male took notice and stopped. More males raced through, some unfamiliar to her. The one who'd paused approached, ignoring Vashti and her brood. He yanked at one of the table's legs, trying to snap it off for a weapon. When that failed, he flipped the table upright, gripped its edge, and slammed its legs against the floor. The wood held firm.

A few more males burst in, seized the one staring at the table, and hauled him out. The stove door creaked open, and the largest child emerged. He watched a long line of males stream through the kitchen. When they'd passed, he glanced at Vashti. She shook her head. He snarled back, scanned the room, spotted an iron utensil— some kitchen tool none of them understood—grabbed it, and chased after the males.

Vashti looked to the table. It was out of reach, unless she left the security of the nook. She wanted to go get it, to pull it to her, to flip it, and cover the hole, but she was afraid. As a substitute she pulled the children against her. They all stared out of the hole together, looking at the table.

A single male stumbled back into the kitchen. He was bleeding. He stopped and leaned against the wall, panting. Blood ran through his fingers, down his body, pooling at his feet. He pushed himself off of the wall and stumbled out of the kitchen.

Vashti heard horrible sounds coming from the direction that the males had run. From the other direction a pair of males entered the kitchen. They were bigger than those who had passed. They wore piecemeal armor and had swords. They did not run, but walked. They were followed by an older male. Vashti recognized him. He had the weird way. He could talk to spirits and could kill with words. She looked away from him. The trio left the kitchen.

She saw bright lights flashing against the walls and floor. Then all was quiet. Some time passed. Her muscles began to ache from holding the children. She relaxed. She sniffed. There was something in the air she had never smelled before. This frightened her.

A stranger entered the kitchen. He was not a goblin. He was a man. Vashti peered out of the hole. She thought of the man trapped in the book. The armor both men wore was similar. She thought that they could be the same man.

She wondered if he had escaped from the paper prison. She wondered if he was angry at having been trapped. She wondered if he would remember her, and spare her. She desperately wanted to check behind the stone, to open the strange prison and look for the man, to confirm her suspicions.

The man, speaking over his shoulder, said something she didn't understand. He lowered his gore-covered sword and entered the kitchen. He walked to the table and set his sword on it. He reached up and took off his helmet. His long hair fell around his shoulders. Vashti saw his almond-shaped eyes. Her heart leapt. 'Free!' She thought. 'Here!' More importantly, he did not seem angry. She almost rushed out of the hole to greet him but a second man entered.

He was different from the man who had been trapped, but who was now free. He was not wearing armor, but a robe. There was a gash in the robe, rimmed with blood, but the man did not act wounded. He held a stick in his hand. The stick glowed, but not with fire. His features were different from the other man's, softer. His ears were pointed, like Vashti's, but not as long. He approached the table. He spoke. Vashti did not comprehend. The first man lifted his sword, flung the blood from it with a sharp downward chop, and put it in his scabbard. The second man pulled out a piece of paper and unrolled it on the table.

A third man entered. No, Vashti corrected herself, it was a woman, but she wore the clothes of a man, pants and armor. She carried a mace in one hand. Blood and gore dripped from its spiked head. An unfamiliar symbol hung from a chain at the woman's neck. It glowed with a faint light. The woman crossed the room and stood in the opposite doorway.

The two men stood at the table, talking. The man in the robe took out a small stick, bent over the paper, and marked on it. Vashti could not see, only guess. She looked among the strangers. She discerned that a fourth had entered. He was crouched in the shadows, looking directly at her. When she spotted him, she shrieked. Several of the children began to cry.

The man in the shadows stepped into the robed one's light. He said something and motioned to the hole. Vashti pulled the children closer. The man who had somehow escaped from the book pulled out his sword. He approached the hole, knelt, and looked in. He waved and the robed man approached, holding his light close.

The two men spoke to each other. The man with the sword reached into the hole. Without thinking, Vashti bit at him. He yanked his hand back. She regretted her action and grew frightened. The man with the light laughed. The man-who-could-hide-like-a-goblin stepped up and placed his hands on the kneeling man's shoulders, speaking. The once-trapped man rose and stepped aside.

The man knelt and began to speak. Vashti was so frightened that her ears failed her.

"...more?" he asked.

She looked at him, not understanding.

"Where?" This was followed by a movement of the lips that Vashti's fear-deafened ears failed to hear, followed by, "Chieftain?"

She looked to the doorway in which stood the strangely dressed woman. The man-that-could-hide-like-a-goblin tossed the food into the hole. It was salted meat, the smell of it filled the small space.

"Eat," he said.

She shook her head. The man with the glowing stick said something and laughed. It was not a kind laugh.

"We won't hurt you," said the kneeling man.

Vashti did not respond. Some of her children cried, some growled, some had been frightened into total silence. None reached for the food, although all wanted it. The man with the glowing stick said something in a harsh tone. The woman spoke to him, arguing. She pointed to the hole.

"If you don't come out my friend will send magic in to get you. Do you know what magic is?"

She looked at him, not understanding.

"You had a shaman."

Still, she did not understand.

"A male that talked to spirits, spoke hexes, performed miracles, something like that. You understand? Yes. My friend is a powerful shaman. He's angry at you for hiding in there. You'd better come out."

Vashti let go of the children. She crawled out of the hole, keeping her eyes on the pointed-eared man with the weird way about him. The children pulled the salted meat to them, tore it into pieces, and began to eat, chewing with exaggerated slowness, not wanting to draw attention.

Vashti stood next to the hole. The man-who-could-hide-like-a-goblin stuck his head into the small space. He pulled it back out and stood up. He said something to the others. The powerful shaman spoke to him.

"He wants to know how many goblins in your tribe?"

She shook her head, not understanding. The two men spoke.

"He wants to know if you have ever seen any other humans here."

Vashti stared at him. She had only seen one man before, the man trapped in the book. She smiled and nodded.

"Good. We're getting somewhere."

Vashti looked to the man with the sword. She studied him, asking herself if he truly was the same man she had seen trapped. It was difficult to tell. She studied his face.

"What is it?" asked the man-who-could-hide-like-a-goblin.

Vashti looked to him. She looked back to the other man. She studied his face further, his mouth, his nose, his eyes, especially his almond-shaped eyes. She thought he was beautiful. He was, to her simple mind, the image of a god. She decided that he had escaped his prison and had come to her.

Without knowing what she was doing, she stepped towards him, reaching out. The man watched her, sword in hand. She arrived at his feet, and gazed up at him. He looked down at her. She reached up, trying to touch his face, as she had done so many times before.

With her other hand she tapped her chest, smiling. She was certain he would recognize her. Had not their eyes met many times? Had she not consoled him in his captivity? Certainly, she felt, he must appreciate the efforts she made, her difficult vigil. She kept him safe from the other goblins. Now he had escaped and she felt she had played a vital role. These emotions were clear in her countenance. She watched as a self-conscious smile spread on the beautiful man's face. He said something to the man who was now behind her.

"What do you want?" the man-who-could-hide-like-a-goblin translated.

She looked to the speaker, then back into those almond-shaped eyes. The man behind her said something. He looked at his companion for some time. Then he looked down at Vashti. He sheathed his sword and knelt down.

Vashti shook with nervousness. She reached out. Her hand hovered close to his cheek. She stared into his cinnamon colored eyes. The woman spoke. She entered the room and stood behind the man with the sword. The man with the glowing stick rolled up the piece of paper, snickered, and looked at Vashti with contempt. He went to the doorway. The woman spoke to the man-who-could-hide-like-a-goblin.

Vashti ignored them. She was building up the courage to touch his face, the face she had touched many times. This time would be different. The man was studying her, looking into her eyes. He reached up. His hand was gloved. He seemed to be reaching for her hand. She felt her opportunity vanishing. She pressed her hand against his cheek. It was soft, despite the stubble, and warm. Tears came to her eyes.

The woman spoke. The once-trapped-man smiled. This made Vashti smile. The movement of her cheeks dropped the tears from her eyes. They cleaned twin trails on her filthy green skin. The man shook his glove from his hand. He reached up and placed his hand over Vashti's.

For a moment they stared into each other's eyes. It was a moment that seemed to last forever for Vashti. Her heart swelled. She began to feel faint. The room began to spin and grew dark. The man caught her as she fell.

. . .

"What do you think that was about?" asked Nefar, the Elven wizard.

Husain held the goblin in his arms. She was no bigger or heavier than a human child.

"She thought he was handsome," answered Brie.

"To think," continued Nefar, "I almost sent a whole mess of magic into that hole." He laughed. "I could have killed your paramour, Husain."

"What are we going to do with them?" asked Brie.

"Why do anything?" answered the thief. "An unarmed female and a bunch of children. They're no threat."

"May I remind you, children goblins grow up to be adult goblins."

"Nefar," Brie looked at him, "That's hardly charitable or noble."

Nefar shrugged his shoulders. "Doesn't make it untrue." He looked down the hall. "We've wasted quite a lot of time on Husain's little romance. I suggest we kill them and keep moving."

"We leave them be," said Brie. "I'm surprised at you, Nefar. Don't make me regret healing you."

"Goblins can't be trusted," he replied, shrugging his shoulders.

The thief looked down at Husain, who was still kneeling, holding the goblin as a man might hold a bride, or a father a child. "You hold her fate in your arms, Husain."

Husain looked up, then looked into the face of the unconscious goblin. "Why did she do that?" he asked. No one answered. He rose, lifting her, and walked to the hole.

"Will they hurt her?" he asked the thief, who was the only among them who knew anything about goblin culture, such as it was.

"If they're hungry enough they might eat her."

Husain looked at the thief.

"I'm kidding."

Husain knelt and placed her before the hole. He rose and walked over to where his glove lay on the floor. He bent and retrieved it. "Let's go." He turned to the thief. "You scout ahead?"

The thief smiled. "Oh, may I?" He laughed then made his way past the party, disappearing into the shadows of the hallway. Not long after the thief left, Brie turned and went into the hall. Nefar followed. Husain began to put his glove on then stopped. Instead, he pulled off his other glove. He walked to the unconscious goblin, knelt, and looked into the hole. "These are hers," he said, holding up the gloves.

He placed the gloves on her stomach and crossed her hands over them. He looked at her, still not understanding her queer behavior. He recalled the emotion that had been in her eyes as she looked into his. He reached out and touched her cheek. For a moment he saw her not as a goblin, but something more, a being with a private inner life. This caused him to feel guilty for having come to the long-abandoned castle, for slaughtering so many of her kind.

The rude noise of chewing and swallowing came to his ears. He glanced into the hole. The children, filthy, half-starved, their eyes filled with animal fear, yet still chewing, shook him from his thoughts. The feeling of compassion passed. He chuckled at himself, rose, drew his sword, and followed the others.

. . .

Vashti woke up. The room was empty and silent. She felt something under her hands. She sat up. She looked into the hole. Her children stared at her. She made sure none were missing. Only the eldest was absent. She looked down.

There, fallen into her lap, were the warrior's gloves. They were warm, even a bit damp. She lifted them to her nose and sniffed. The aroma, his aroma, was so intense she began to feel faint again.

She stood, rushed to a chair, dragged it to the stove, scrambled onto the shelf, across the shelf to the stone, worked the stone free, and pulled out the strange object. She opened it and found him. He was still there. She looked around the room.

"Man? Man!" she yelled. She looked down at the hole. Her children stuck their heads out and were now watching their mother's frantic actions. Her youngest daughter gleamed some notion of what her mother was wanting. Her skinny arm emerged from the hole. She pointed down the hall.

"Man?" asked Vashti, holding out the gloves.

The children nodded in unison.

Vashti looked back to the illustration. She found the warrior's hands. He was not wearing gloves. She could not remember, though she try, if he was wearing gloves before.

She decided that he had been. Now, his hands were bare, and she had the gloves. She touched the page, her eyes closed. She knew what his face felt like; soft, despite the stubble, and warm.

She closed the book and stuffed it back into the hole. She stuffed the gloves into the hole, on top of the book, then set the stone back in place. She climbed down, grabbed the table, turned it on its side, and drug it to the hole. She climbed in, pulled the table as close to the hole as she could, pulled her children to her, and sat in the darkness.

Her children could not see her smiling.

The Wisdom of the Ancients

"What of *him*?" The hobgoblin general, Gruffyd, waved toward the closed pavilion door-flap, motioning to the recently dismissed messenger sent by his peer and rival, General Yago. "Why does my rival send that?" He pointed to the letter in Ieuan's hands. "Read it."

Gruffyd sat cross-legged on a ram's pelt in his field pavilion in the heart of his camp, surrounded by his *Ten Thousand*. His shaman, Ieuan, and his chief military advisors, Ryd and Nai, sat with him. At his right-hand was the crippled and blind old veteran, Cedig.

Ieuan unfolded the parchment and tilted it towards the ray of sunlight angling through the dust from the open smoke-letting-flap above. "Victory to you," read Ieuan. "The hated orcs fear your name. They fear your scarlet banner. They fear the pounding of your men's boots upon the cracked earth. They fear your *Ten Thousand*."

"Whose words are these?" asked Gruffyd, laughing.

"Maybe they've an elven poet as a prisoner of war," said Ryd.

"They must," said Nai.

"Go on," said the general.

"I would send emissaries to you to learn your ways, for your glory shall be shared amongst us all. The hobgoblin tribes shall slay the orcs. Share your power, Gruffyd. Share the wisdom of the ancients."

"An elven poet," grumbled Ryd. "To be sure."

"He hides behind words," said Gruffyd, leaning forward. Ieuan handed him the letter. Gruffyd examined it, although he could not read. He tossed the letter on the ground before him. "He would steal my power."

"Deny him," said Nai.

"Better yet," added Ryd, "send this letter back—soaked in blood."

"Maglubiyet curse this trick," said the shaman, spitting on the parchment.

A moment's silence passed. In it Gruffyd pondered the meaning of Yago's letter.

"In days that Yago must think ancient," began Cedig, "indeed, in which most of the *Ten Thousand* would deem long past, we used to polish our bronze armor to a high shine. The sun would reflect from our breastplates, helmets, and shields. What must we have looked like in the midday sun? Did we not shine like the soldiers of god? As if Maglubiyet himself stood with us? More than once this alone was enough to turn our enemy from the field of battle."

Gruffyd looked from the scarred face of the old veteran, with its closed eyelids that hid unseeing eyes, to the faces of his advisors and shaman. He turned back to Cedig.

"Why tell us this?"

"Let them come," said Cedig. "Let them see you have no fear. Let them see the sun shining from your armor. Yago will doubt his ability to topple you when his emissaries return in awe of your might."

. . .

The trio of emissaries bowed their heads to the pelt-carpeted floor of Gruffyd's pavilion. They had brought gifts; a suit of elven chainmail taken in battle, an axe the height and weight of a hobgoblin, said to have belonged to the giant, Inir, and a trunk full of gold and silver coins from conquered lands.

They were full of flowery speech, which Gruffyd listened to with a wry smile. He rose and, along with his advisors and shaman, led the emissaries from the pavilion. Cedig did not follow. He sat alone in the pavilion for a while then rose and, with the help of a slave, went to his own pavilion.

His body-slave was washing Cedig's feet—he had dined and was preparing to retire early—when the three emissaries entered and begged an audience. They were accompanied by a guard. Cedig motioned that they should sit.

"Great is General Gruffyd," said one of the emissaries.

"Aye," agreed Cedig.

"Great are the *Ten Thousand*," said another.

"Aye."

A moment's silence passed.

"We have heard of your greatness, too," said the final emissary. "It is believed that Gruffyd's true power comes from your wisdom."

Cedig thought for a moment. "How could a blind and crippled veteran be of help? I'm a relic, nothing more."

"Did you hear General Yago's letter read aloud?" asked the first emissary to speak. Cedig nodded. "When we said we wished to learn the wisdom of the ancients, we meant you."

Cedig laughed. "Ancient, eh?"

"We meant no disrespect," said the third emissary.

"Tell us, what was battle like when you were young?" asked the second emissary.

Cedig laughed. "Not like today." He shook his head. "There were no long, drawn out campaigns. There were no missile-throwers; no javelins, no slings. We did not use cavalry. There were no skirmishers."

"Only infantry?" asked one of the emissaries.

Cedig nodded. "We gathered together in a phalanx, much like today, but we were equipped—severely."

"How so?" asked another.

"We wore what was called panoply. This consisted of a bronze breastplate, quite heavy, a bronze helm that covered the ears and face." He laughed. "One could barely see out of it—or drawn a breath. Also greaves. Most important was our shield and spear. We packed together eight ranks deep.

"Each man sought protection beneath not his own shield but the one to his right. Each man protected not himself but his companion to the left. In that way we were linked together, that is, we had a reason to maintain our formation. In our right hand we carried our spears. We had short swords, too, for when our spears shattered."

"But why no missile-throwers? Why no cavalry or skirmishers?" asked one of the emissaries. "These have value on the field of battle."

"Aye," agreed Cedig. "In a long campaign they're needed, especially against orcs. But *we* did not need them. You see, we fought ourselves then—tribe against tribe, hobgoblin against hobgoblin. You might wonder why this meant we used only infantry: I will tell you.

"This was before the massive armies of today. The tribes were small and scattered. What was the use of a long campaign? We had crops to tend, animals to keep, children to rear. No, what was best was one decisive battle. You see, we fought by agreement. We could have used missile-throwers, skirmishers, and even cavalry, but why?"

He shook his head. "Why waste our time, our resources? Why labor in the field of battle for weeks or months when our own fields needed tilling? One decisive battle was best." He rubbed his chin. "It was more than that. You see, Maglubiyet himself wanted," here he paused to compose his thoughts, "one pure moment of courage. In that moment, when the two sides clashed, he would see which tribe was fearless and which held fear in their hearts.

"Maglubiyet would favor the courageous. A multitude of seeds would come from one. Each babe, be it a piglet or a hobgoblin, would be full of vigor. No illness, no waste or want. Such was the favor won in that brief moment of terror and bloodshed."

The three emissaries looked at one another, hesitating.

"Great is your wisdom," said one. Although they spoke praise, they drew their daggers. One held a hand crossbow low against his side and fitted a poison-coated dart. This was for the guard who stood by the pavilion's door-flap. Of course, Cedig could not see this. The guard could not either, for the assassins were skilled in sleight-of-hand.

"Would you like to know how I became crippled and blind?" asked Cedig. The three emissaries, who were really three assassins sent to kill him, paused. "I cannot say how many seasons have passed since my last battle—too many. I was in the second line, my shield against the back of the man in front of me, my spear at his side. We had clashed hard with the enemy and the ranks were coming apart like a badly sewn coat. There was much death and dying. Men were beneath my feet. My spear had shattered in the first collision."

He rubbed his thighs. "An enemy spear entered here." He patted the outside of his left thigh. "And exited here." He patted the outside of his right thigh. "I can't say how I kept my feet beneath me. I thought for certain I was going down and that I would be trampled by my kinsmen. I remember," he held out his hand, indicating his left side.

"A massive hoplite strode up next to me. By then my strength was failing. I had dropped my shield. I knew I was soon to die. This hoplite, I remember his armor was black, not polished bronze like mine, he stood a foot taller than me and must have weighed twice as much, so broad was his back. He had neither spear nor sword, not even a shield. He grabbed the soldier about to strike my life from me, lifted him overhead—remember our breastplate alone was fifty pounds—and hurled him backwards into his own ranks."

The three assassins looked at one another, unbelieving. They wondered if perhaps the old veteran was insane. They began to question the need to slay him.

"He turned to me," continued Cedig. "He was laughing. I looked into his face. His skin was as black as a piece of ebony. His eyes were fire."

"Maglubiyet?" whispered one of the assassins.

"Yes," said Cedig, nodding. "It was our god, the god of war. When my gaze met his I was struck blind. For the rest of my life I shall see only his blood-spattered face, his fire-bright eyes. Although I hear you speak now I must listen hard, for my ears ring with his battle-laughter. You seek the wisdom of the ancients? It's this: it matters not if one has missile-throwers, cavalry, or skirmishers. What an army needs for victory is courage—one must laugh in the face of death."

The three assassins looked at one another, then to Cedig.

"Yes," said one, starting to rise, his dagger advancing. "Gruffyd gets his power from you." The other assassins began their grim tasks. The hand crossbow was leveled. The guard was shocked by its sudden appearance. The second dagger was quick to parallel the first.

Cedig tilted his face up toward those of his would-be murderers, who now stood over him. His greenish-gray skin turned as black as ebony. He opened his eyes. They were made of fire. The bright light of them flashed hot in the faces of the three assassins. In the heat of his gaze their bowels turned to liquid, their courage to cowardice. They dropped their weapons and raced from the pavilion, half-tripping over Cedig's body-slave, who had been curled up asleep, and pushed past the guard, who turned to chase them.

Cedig closed his eyes. He breathed deeply, then bent forward and felt for the weapons. He touched them with the tips of his fingers and laughed.

H. Rad Bethlen has been compared to Isak Dinesen (*Seven Gothic Tales*) and Fritz Leiber (*Swords and Deviltry*). He is known for his work in the fantasy and horror genres as well as his non-fiction. He has been published in Europe and America.

Enjoy these stories?

If you liked what you read, please take a moment to **leave a review on Amazon**! Your feedback helps other readers find these stories. It only takes a minute but it makes a huge difference. The Amazon algorithm requires 30-50 reviews before it will pick this book up and promote it to like-minded readers. Your review is instrumental in helping that happen!

For more great fiction and non-fiction please visit:

roosterandravenpublishing.com

hradbethlen.com

or H. Rad Bethlen's Amazon page.

www.ingramcontent.com/pod-product-compliance
Lightning Source LLC
Chambersburg PA
CBHW070652130626
46555CB00006B/2847